Team Spirit

THE CHICAGO BEARS

BY
MARK STEWART

Content Consultant
Jason Aikens
Collections Curator
The Professional Football Hall of Fame

NorwoodHouse Press
Chicago, Illinois

Norwood House Press
P.O. Box 316598
Chicago, Illinois 60631

For information regarding Norwood House Press, please visit our website at:
www.norwoodhousepress.com or call 866-565-2900.

PHOTO CREDITS:
All photos courtesy of AP Images—AP/Wide World Photos, Inc. except the following:
Jim McIsaac/Getty Images (cover); Author's Collection (6 & 34 right);
Arthur Rickerby (7); Author's Collection/Little Brown (26); TCMA, Inc. (14);
Goudey Gum Co. (16); National Chicle (20 & 34 left);
Topps, Inc. (21 both, 22, 30, 31, 40 both & 43);
Black Book Archives (28, 35 top right, 36 & 41 both);
Red Label Records (29); Fran Byrne Photography (39).
Special thanks to Topps, Inc.

Editor: Mike Kennedy
Associate Editor: Brian Fitzgerald
Designer: Ron Jaffe
Project Management: Black Book Partners, LLC.
Special thanks to: Pam and Richard Donath, Bobby Hall and Bruce Kaminski

LIBRARY OF CONGRESS CATALOGING-IN-PUBLICATION DATA

Stewart, Mark, 1960-
The Chicago Bears / by Mark Stewart ; content consultant Jason Aikens.
p. cm. -- (Team spirit)
Summary: "Presents the history, accomplishments and key personalities of the Chicago Bears football team. Includes timelines, quotes, maps, glossary and websites"--Provided by publisher.
Includes bibliographical references and index.
ISBN-13: 978-1-59953-121-2 (library edition : alk. paper)
ISBN-10: 1-59953-121-6 (library edition : alk. paper)
1. Chicago Bears (Football team)--History--Juvenile literature. I. Aikens, Jason. II. Title.
GV956.C5S74 2008
796.332'64'0977311--dc22

2007007500

Manufactured in the United States of America.

COVER PHOTO: The Bears celebrate a touchdown during a victory in the 2006 season.

Table of Contents

SPORTS WORDS & VOCABULARY WORDS: In this book, you will find many words that are new to you. You may also see familiar words used in new ways. The glossary on page 46 gives the meanings of football words, as well as "everyday" words that have special football meanings. These words appear in **bold type** throughout the book. The glossary on page 47 gives the meanings of vocabulary words that are not related to football. They appear in ***bold italic type*** throughout the book.

Meet the Bears

In the early days of the **National Football League (NFL)**, teams searched for nicknames that captured the spirit of the sport. The city of Chicago grabbed one of the best and called its club the Bears. Few animals are as fast, powerful, rugged, and ***persistent.*** These are the same qualities Chicago coaches look for in their players.

The Bears have had some wonderful runners, passers, and receivers over the years. Yet they have never forgotten the basics. In the NFL, you win by **blocking** and tackling better than your opponent. Even in today's modern game, most of the Bears' victories come the "old-fashioned" way.

This book tells the story of the Bears. Their past is part of the history of football in America. Their present is a reminder that a great, hard-hitting defense is still the key to winning close games. And their future is brighter than ever.

Cedric Benson is congratulated by teammates after scoring a touchdown.
The Bears love playing in Chicago's cold winter weather.

Way Back When

Professional football was not always as popular as it is today. In the early 1900s, few fans cared about the sport at all. This changed thanks to a group of businessmen led by George Halas, who ran a team called the Decatur Staleys. He and the others formed the **American Professional Football Association (APFA)** in 1920. Two years later, Halas convinced his fellow owners to call the APFA the National Football League.

By then, Halas had moved his team to Chicago and renamed it the Bears. They became a ***sensation*** in 1925 after adding Red Grange. Nicknamed the "Galloping Ghost," he thrilled fans with long touchdown runs through crowds of tacklers. After Grange's first season, Halas took his Bears on a coast-to-coast **exhibition tour** that helped pro football gain national popularity.

During the 1930s, Halas built his team into a powerhouse. The Bears won the **NFL Championship** in 1932 and 1933, and reached the title game in 1934 and 1937. Chicago's best player was Bronko

Nagurski, an enormous runner who blasted through defenses. He was joined by three talented **linemen**—George Musso, Danny Fortmann, and Joe Stydahar—and an end named Bill Hewitt, one of the last NFL stars to play without a helmet.

The Bears were even better in the 1940s. Quarterback Sid Luckman teamed up with center Bulldog Turner, running back George McAfee, and receiver Ken Kavanaugh to make the Bears almost unstoppable. They played for the NFL Championship every year from 1940 to 1943 and again in 1946. During the 1950s, the Bears finished first or second in their **division** six times. Their stars included Johnny Lujack, George Connor, Bill George, Harlon Hill, Stan Jones, Doug Atkins, Willie Galimore, and Rick Casares.

Many of these great players were still on the team in 1963, when Chicago won another NFL Championship. Later in the ***decade***, the Bears had two of the NFL's most remarkable stars, Dick Butkus and Gale Sayers. Butkus was the most feared tackler in football. Sayers

LEFT: Red Grange is shown on a 1929 poster.
ABOVE: Dick Butkus grips his helmet and George Halas hurries down the sideline, as Gale Sayers runs toward the end zone.

Wilson
34

had the best moves of any running back in the NFL. Another star for Chicago in the 1960s was tight end Mike Ditka.

In 1982, Halas hired Ditka to coach the Bears. They won 15 games in 1985 and went on to win the **Super Bowl**. Their leaders were running back Walter Payton, quarterback Jim McMahon, and defensive stars Mike Singletary, Dan Hampton, Steve McMichael, and Richard Dent. Payton was the perfect combination of speed, power, and toughness. Chicago's defense was the most fearsome in the league.

The Bears continued their ***tradition*** of hard-hitting defense during the 1990s. Chicago had many good years but fell short of reaching a second Super Bowl. It would take a new generation of Bears to bring the team back to the big game.

LEFT: Walter Payton sidesteps a tackle. He was one of the hardest players in the NFL to bring down. **ABOVE**: Richard Dent and Mike Singletary

31
54

The Team Today

The Bears figured out long ago what it takes to build a championship team. The process begins with a great defense that plays hard and smart in the key moments of close games. In 2000, the Bears **drafted** Brian Urlacher, who quickly became their defensive leader. Chicago continued adding pieces to the puzzle, including Lance Briggs, Nathan Vasher, Tommie Harris, and special teams star Devin Hester.

On offense, the Bears brought together a group of talented players including Cedric Benson, Rex Grossman, Olin Kreutz, Desmond Clark, Muhsin Muhammad, Robbie Gould, and Ruben Brown. They made the most of the opportunities the defense gave them.

Under head coach Lovie Smith, the Bears went from the bottom of the **North Division** in the **National Football Conference (NFC)** to the top in just one season. In 2006, they finished with the best record in the NFC. The Bears then defeated the Seattle Seahawks and New Orleans Saints in the **playoffs** to reach the Super Bowl for the second time in team history.

Brian Urlacher raises his arm in celebration as Nathan Vasher scores a touchdown for the defense.

BEARS

Home Turf

Starting in 1921, the Bears shared Wrigley Field with the Chicago Cubs baseball club. In 1971, the team moved to Soldier Field in downtown Chicago. The stadium honors men and women who have fought in wars for America.

When the temperature drops in December, no one wants to play the Bears at Soldier Field. The stadium is located close to Lake Michigan. The wind often whips off the water, making it very chilly and uncomfortable for visiting players. On days like these, the weather is like a "12th player" for the Bears.

In 2002, Soldier Field was modernized. Many Chicagoans were sad to see the old stadium change. But when Soldier Field reopened in 2003, it ranked among America's best new buildings.

BY THE NUMBERS

- *There are 61,500 seats for football at Soldier Field.*
- *Soldier Field opened in 1924. It was known as Grant Park Municipal Stadium.*
- *The Bears beat the Pittsburgh Steelers 17–15 in the first game at Soldier Field, on September 19, 1971.*
- *In 1927, more than 123,000 fans jammed into the stadium for a college football game.*

Four jets from the Michigan Air National Guard fly over Soldier Field before a Bears playoff game in 2006.

Dressed for Success

When George Halas designed his team's first uniforms, he chose navy blue and orange. Those were the colors of his college, the University of Illinois. During the 1920s and 1930s, the Bears wore blue jerseys with orange stripes or orange jerseys with blue stripes. Often, the stripes were made of ***canvas***, which helped players carry the football without **fumbling**. In the 1940s, the team began using the deep, almost blackish blue and orange colors it wears today. By the early 1950s, stripes had been added to the sleeves, pants, and socks. In 1970, player names appeared on the backs of the uniforms.

The Bears used several different helmet colors over the years, including brown, black, blue, and white. In 1962, they added a large wishbone-shaped C to each side of their helmets. The team's mascot, of course, is a bear. Chicago has featured different bears on its pennants and programs since the 1920s.

Rick Casares models the team's uniform from the 1950s.

UNIFORM BASICS

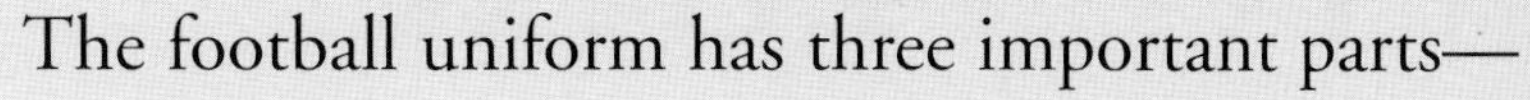

The football uniform has three important parts—

- Helmet
- Jersey
- Pants

Helmets used to be made out of leather, and they did not have facemasks—ouch! Today, helmets are made of super-strong plastic. The uniform top, or jersey, is made of thick fabric. It fits snugly around a player so that tacklers cannot grab it and pull him down. The pants come down just over the knees.

There is a lot more to a football uniform than what you see on the outside. Air can be pumped inside the helmet to give it a snug, padded fit. The jersey covers shoulder pads, and sometimes a rib protector called a flak jacket. The pants include pads that protect the hips, thighs, ***tailbone***, and knees.

Football teams have two sets of uniforms—one dark and one light. This makes it easier to tell two teams apart on the field. Almost all teams wear their dark uniforms at home and their light ones on the road.

Lance Briggs wears Chicago's 2006 uniform. The Bears have had the same team colors for many years.

We Won!

The Bears won their first championship in 1921, when they were known as the Chicago Staleys. That season, there was no championship game. When the Bears finished first in the league with nine wins, one loss and one tie, they were crowned champions. **Player-coach** George Halas guided a talented team that included George Trafton and Guy Chamberlain.

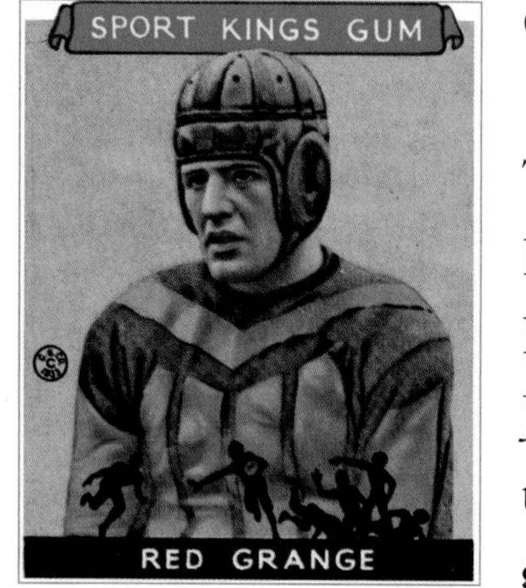

Chicago's next championship came in 1932. The NFL was a low-scoring league, except for the Bears. Among Chicago's offensive stars were Bronko Nagurski, Red Grange, Bill Hewitt, Luke Johnsos, and Keith Molesworth. The Bears beat the Portsmouth Spartans 9–0 in a special playoff game for the championship.

The following year, the NFL was divided into two divisions, East and West. The league scheduled a championship game between the division winners. The Bears faced the New York Giants in the league's first official title contest. Chicago won 23–21 on a great play in the fourth quarter. Hewitt caught a short pass from Nagurski, then pitched the ball to Bill Karr, who ran the rest of the way for the winning touchdown.

The Bears won the NFL West in 1934 and 1937 but lost in the championship games both times. In 1940, Halas ***assembled*** a new squad led by quarterback Sid Luckman, lightning-fast runner George McAfee, and Bulldog Turner, a great center and linebacker. Chicago met the Washington Redskins for the title and wiped them out 73-0!

The Bears took the league championship again in 1941, 1943, and 1946. After Luckman retired, the Bears slowly rebuilt their team. In 1963, they won the NFL Championship again. That club was known for its great defense, which was led by Bill George, Ed O'Bradovich, Doug Atkins, and Richie Petitbon. The Bears gave up just 144 points during the regular season, then defeated the Giants 14–10 for their eighth NFL Championship.

Chicago fans had to wait more than 20 years for their next NFL Championship, but it was worth it. The 1985 Bears were one of the best teams ever. They had many excellent players on offense, including Walter Payton, Jim McMahon, and linemen Jim Covert

LEFT: Red Grange, a star of the 1932 championship team.
ABOVE: Sid Luckman, George McAfee, and Ray McLean celebrate the team's 1946 championship.

34
GSH
60

and Jay Hilgenberg. Chicago was even better when its opponents had the ball. Linebacker Mike Singletary was the leader of a unit that squeezed the life out of its enemies. Other defensive stars included Otis Wilson, Gary Fencik, Dave Duerson, Dan Hampton, Richard Dent, and a gigantic **rookie** named William Perry. They all loved the attacking system created by Buddy Ryan, the coach in charge of the defense.

The Bears finished the 1985 season 15–1 under head coach Mike Ditka. In the playoffs, they shut out the Giants and the Los Angeles Rams. Then in Super Bowl XX, Chicago whipped the New England Patriots. McMahon completed several long passes to receiver Willie Gault, while Payton led a running attack that gained 167 yards. On defense, Singletary and Dent punished the Patriots whenever they had the ball.

The score was 37–3 in the third quarter when McMahon handed off to Perry, who was in the game on a special goal-line play. Perry slammed the door on New England with a one-yard touchdown run. The final score was 46–10.

LEFT: The Patriots struggle to catch Walter Payton during Super Bowl XX. The initials on his sleeve stand for George S. Halas, who passed away in 1983. **ABOVE**: William Perry spikes the ball after his Super Bowl touchdown. The huge defensive tackle was known as "The Fridge."

Go-To Guys

To be a true star in the NFL, you need more than fast feet and a big body. You have to be a "go-to guy"—someone the coach wants on the field at the end of a big game. Bears fans have had a lot to cheer about over the years, including these great stars …

THE PIONEERS

RED GRANGE — Running Back/Defensive Back

- Born: 6/13/1903 • Died: 1/28/1991
- Played for Team: 1925 & 1929 to 1934

Red Grange was the NFL's first true superstar. After his first season with the Bears, he went on a coast-to-coast exhibition tour with other top players. More than 400,000 fans bought tickets to watch Grange play.

BRONKO NAGURSKI — Running Back/Linebacker

- Born: 11/3/1908 • Died: 1/7/1990
- Played for Team: 1930 to 1937 & 1943

Bronko Nagurski was the heart of the Bears during the 1930s. He could run, pass, block, and tackle as well as anyone in the NFL. Nagurski left football after eight seasons to become a professional wrestler. He later returned to the Bears and helped them win the 1943 championship.

SID LUCKMAN — Quarterback

• Born: 11/21/1916 • Died: 7/5/1998 • Played for Team: 1939 to 1950

George Halas believed the T-formation was the future of football, but he needed a quarterback to master it. Sid Luckman was his man. Luckman led the NFL in passing yards and touchdowns three times and guided the Bears to four championships during the 1940s.

BILL GEORGE — Linebacker

• Born: 10/27/1929 • Died: 9/30/1982

• Played for Team: 1952 to 1965

Bill George was the key to Chicago's ferocious defense in the 1950s and early 1960s. His ability to stop running backs in their tracks and cover pass receivers made him the NFL's first great middle linebacker.

MIKE DITKA — Tight End

• Born: 10/18/1939 • Played for Team: 1961 to 1966

When Mike Ditka joined the Bears, he showed that a tight end could be an excellent blocker *and* receiver. He took opponents by surprise as a rookie by catching 56 passes for 1,076 yards and 12 touchdowns. Later, he coached the Bears to the 1985 championship.

LEFT: Bronko Nagurski
TOP RIGHT: Bill George **BOTTOM RIGHT**: Mike Ditka

MODERN STARS

DICK BUTKUS — Linebacker

- Born: 12/9/1942
- Played for Team: 1965 to 1973

For nine seasons during the 1960s and 1970s, Dick Butkus played with anger, passion, and an ***intense*** desire to win. He scared opponents with his hard tackling style but was beloved by Bears fans for his fearless play.

GALE SAYERS — Running Back

- Born: 5/30/1943
- Played for Team: 1965 to 1971

Gale Sayers was known as the "Kansas Comet" because of his amazing speed. He could also stop, change direction, and then restart before the defense had time to react. Sayers once scored six touchdowns in a game against the San Francisco 49ers.

WALTER PAYTON — Running Back

- Born: 7/25/1954 • Died: 11/1/1999 • Played for Team: 1975 to 1987

Walter Payton loved a hard-hitting football game—probably because he often hit tacklers harder than they hit him. Payton's quickness and strength helped him lead the NFC in rushing five years in a row. His friendly, soft-spoken nature earned him the nickname "Sweetness."

LEFT: Dick Butkus **TOP RIGHT**: Dan Hampton
BOTTOM RIGHT: Brian Urlacher

DAN HAMPTON Defensive Lineman

• BORN: 9/19/1957 • PLAYED FOR TEAM: 1979 TO 1990

Dan Hampton made life very difficult for opponents and made playing defense very fun for the Bears. He often tied up two or three blockers, which allowed his teammates to swarm the ball carrier. Hampton stood 6' 5", weighed 265 pounds, and was nicknamed "Danimal."

MIKE SINGLETARY Linebacker

• BORN: 10/9/1958 • PLAYED FOR TEAM: 1981 TO 1992

Mike Singletary played defense with great energy and intensity. He seemed to be everywhere at once. Singletary was the kind of leader a defense needs—he never quit on a play and took it personally whenever an opponent scored.

BRIAN URLACHER Linebacker

• BORN: 5/25/1978 • FIRST SEASON WITH TEAM: 2000

The Bears have built their defensive tradition around great linebackers. When Brian Urlacher joined the team, Chicago fans had a ***hunch*** that they were headed back to the Super Bowl. They were right. The Bears made it all the way to the big game in 2007.

On the Sidelines

For more than 60 years, the most important man on the field and off it for Chicago was George "Papa Bear" Halas. He owned the team beginning in 1921 and coached the Bears for 40 seasons. In all, Halas won 318 regular-season games. He was the first coach to hold daily practices, study game film of opponents, and hire special assistants to help run the team.

When Halas was unable to work on the sidelines, he handpicked some excellent coaches for the Bears. Ralph Jones, Hunk Anderson, Paddy Driscoll, and Mike Ditka all won championships in Chicago. Ditka's victory in Super Bowl XX came two years after Halas passed away. Many were surprised that Halas hired him. When Ditka played for the Bears, he and Halas often got into shouting matches. However, Halas knew that Ditka was as passionate about winning as he was.

Halas never met Lovie Smith, but he probably would have liked him. Smith was one of the smartest defensive coaches in the NFL before coming to Chicago in 2004. He led the Bears to the Super Bowl in his third season as the team's head coach.

Lovie Smith, the 2005 NFL Coach of the Year.

One Great Day

DECEMBER 8, 1940

The 36,034 fans who took their seats for the 1940 NFL Championship game expected a defensive battle between the home-team Washington Redskins and the visiting Bears. A few weeks earlier, on the very same field, Washington had beaten Chicago 7–3.

That game ended on an **incomplete pass** from Sid Luckman to Bill Osmanski at the goal line. The Bears argued that the Redskins had **interfered** with Osmanski, but the referee did not see it that way.

Afterwards, George Preston Marshall, the Redskins' owner, told newspaper reporters that the Bears were "quitters" and "crybabies." The Washington players could not believe their ears. The Bears were a great team—there was no reason to make them angry.

The Bears returned to Washington looking for revenge. Coach George Halas and assistant Clark Shaughnessy had been teaching the team the new T-formation, which made it very difficult to tell whether

Chicago was going to run or pass. On the second play of the game, Osmanski sprinted 68 yards for a touchdown. The next time the Bears had the ball, Luckman led them into the end zone on a 17-play **drive**. Chicago scored twice more in the first half, on a 42-yard run by Joe Maniaci and a 30-yard pass from Luckman to Ken Kavanaugh.

The Chicago defense was terrific that day, too. In the third quarter, Hamp Pool, George McAfee, and Bulldog Turner each returned an **interception** for a touchdown. The final score was 73–0.

Not only had the Bears made the Redskins' owner eat his words, they had done so with millions of fans listening in. The 1940 NFL Championship was the first pro football title game ever broadcast coast-to-coast on radio.

LEFT: Sid Luckman, who "wrote the book" on passing.
ABOVE: The scoreboard in Washington tells the story. The Bears are ahead 60–0 with more than 10 minutes left in the game.

Legend Has It

Who was the greatest player in the history of the Pro Bowl?

LEGEND HAS IT that Gale Sayers was. Each year, football's best players gather for a final "all-star" game. Although the **Pro Bowl** is just an exhibition and does not count in the standings, winning is a matter of pride. In 1967, 1968, and 1970, Sayers was the star of stars. His greatest performance came in 1967, when he led the East team to a 20–10 victory. He ran for 110 yards on 11 carries—and also had runs of 55 and 80 yards wiped out by penalties.

ABOVE: Gale Sayers, still one of the most beloved Bears.
RIGHT: Willie Gault (#83) is one of the Bears on the cover of "The Super Bowl Shuffle."

How long was the NFL's shortest field?

LEGEND HAS IT that it was 60 yards. In December 1932, the Bears were scheduled to host a game to break a first-place tie with the Portsmouth Spartans for the NFL title. A heavy snowstorm made it impossible to play outdoors, so the game was moved indoors to Chicago Stadium. To fit in this space, the field was "shrunk" from 100 yards to 60 yards, and the end zones were shaped like half-moons. The Bears did not mind—they won 9–0.

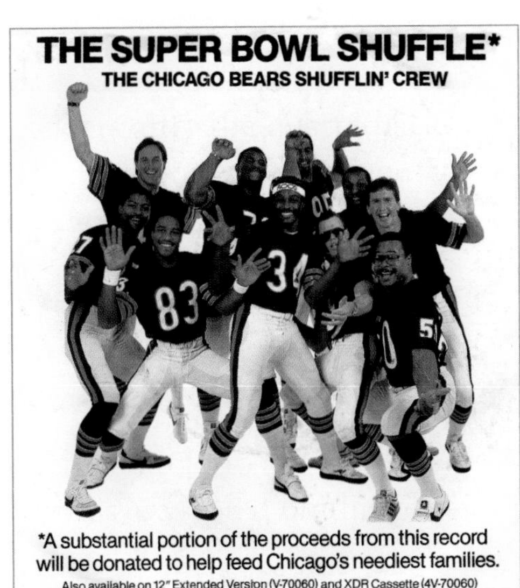

Which team made football's first rap video?

LEGEND HAS IT that the Bears did. During Chicago's amazing 1985 season, receiver Willie Gault convinced several teammates to record a rap song called "The Super Bowl Shuffle." They also made a video to go with it. Two of the team's stars, Walter Payton and Jim McMahon, were not available for the filming, so their parts were ***spliced*** in later. "The Super Bowl Shuffle" was a big hit, and much of the money it generated went to charity. A few months later, the song was nominated for a ***Grammy Award***.

It Really Happened

The Bears have been football pioneers since they first took the field in the 1920s. Over the years, the team brought many important changes to the NFL. In 1967, the Bears decided to change the game again. The team asked two running backs, Gale Sayers and Brian Piccolo, to be roommates that year. Sayers was African-American and Piccolo was white. Never before had an NFL team had interracial roommates. The Bears knew this "experiment" would require two very special people.

Sayers was the NFL's most exciting runner. Piccolo had been a star in college but was not drafted because he was thought to be too small and too slow to make it in the NFL. Sayers and Piccolo shared a hotel room during training camp and on road trips, and the two became great friends. Sayers challenged Piccolo to become a starting player, and he did. When Sayers suffered torn knee ***ligaments*** in 1968, Piccolo challenged him to become the first player to make a complete comeback from that type of injury. In 1969, Sayers returned to the Bears and led the NFL in rushing.

That season should have been one of triumph for the two friends. Instead, it turned out to be tragic. Piccolo was suffering from a bad cough, and when he went to the doctor, he was told that he had lung cancer. Sayers was by his side as he battled the disease, but Piccolo died the following spring.

In 1971, the film *Brian's Song* was made for television. It showed the uplifting friendship between the two players—and the heartbreaking loss suffered by Sayers and his teammates.

LEFT: Brian Piccolo
ABOVE: Gale Sayers

Team Spirit

Most football fans wonder what it might be like to play for their favorite team. Bears fans often seem as if they are ready to hop out of the stands, pull on a helmet and pads, and get into the game. They are tough and dedicated—and they never give up. If the Bears can play in ***searing*** heat or driving snow, Chicago fans can take it, too!

Bears fans live all over the United States—and all over the world. On Sundays, they gather together to watch their team play on TV. In Chicago, game day is a reason to eat, shout, have fun, and remember the team's great moments and players.

At Soldier Field, the fans are stirred to action by the Chicago Bears Drum Corps, the team's official drumline. They also cheer for Staley Da Bear. He is the perfect mascot for the club that so many fans fondly call "Da Bears." His first name also has a special meaning. When the team first came to Chicago, it was named the Staleys. A year later, the Staleys became the Bears.

Bears fans are not shy about showing their loyalty to the team. They roar with delight whenever the Bears win a game.

Timeline

In this timeline, each Super Bowl is listed under the year it was played. Remember that the Super Bowl is held early in the year and is actually part of the previous season. For example, Super Bowl XLI was played on February 4th, 2007, but it was the championship of the 2006 NFL season.

1920
The team plays its first season as the Decatur Staleys.

1934
Beattie Feathers becomes the first player to rush for 1,000 yards.

1946
The Bears win their fourth championship of the 1940s.

1956
Rick Casares leads the NFL in rushing.

1963
The Bears capture their eighth NFL Championship.

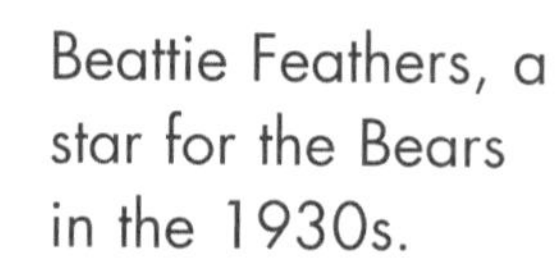
Beattie Feathers, a star for the Bears in the 1930s.

A souvenir pin from the 1940s.

Coach Mike Ditka is carried off the field after Super Bowl XX.

Brian Urlacher does battle with the Tampa Bay Buccaneers.

1972
Bobby Douglass sets a record for quarterbacks with 968 rushing yards.

1980
Walter Payton leads the NFC in rushing for the fifth year in a row.

1986
The Bears win Super Bowl XX.

2005
Brian Urlacher is named Defensive Player of the Year.

2007
The Bears reach the Super Bowl for the second time.

Devin Hester returns the opening kickoff of Super Bowl XLI for a touchdown. Despite this quick score, the Bears lost 29–17.

Fun Facts

SWEET TRICKS

The Bears knew Walter Payton was an unusual player from the moment he arrived at his first training camp in 1975. That summer, he impressed teammates and coaches by catching punts behind his back and walking the length of the field on his hands.

MY HERO

When Chris Zorich took the field with Mike Singletary in the early 1990s, it was a dream come true. As a kid growing up in Chicago, Zorich cheered for the Bears and Singletary was his hero.

FAST TIMES

One of the greatest athletes to wear a Bears uniform was Willie Gault. He would have run in the 1980 Summer ***Olympics*** as a sprinter and hurdler, but the United States did not send a team. Gault later competed in the Winter Olympics as a member of the U.S. bobsled team.

ABOVE: Chris Zorich
RIGHT: The Bears celebrate a big play during the "Fog Bowl."

FOOTBALL FIRST

When Willie Thrower played for the Bears in 1953, he became the NFL's first African-American quarterback. Thrower had led Michigan State University to the **National Championship** the year before.

DID YOU SEE THAT?

On New Year's Eve in 1988, the Bears beat the Philadelphia Eagles 20–12 in a playoff game at Soldier Field. The fog off Lake Michigan made it hard for the fans to see the action—and for the players to see each other. The game is now known as the "Fog Bowl."

WHAT'S UP, DOC?

One of the Bears' smartest linemen was Danny Fortmann. He graduated from college at age 19 and became the NFL's youngest starter as a rookie in 1936. Fortmann attended medical school while playing for Chicago and later became a doctor.

Talking Football

"There's no way I would have made the **Hall of Fame** or set any of the records I did by myself. No matter how many yards I gained, whether it was three or three hundred, someone had to be there to make the block."

—Gale Sayers, on his great Chicago teammates

"I want to be remembered as the guy who gave his all whenever he was on the field."

—Walter Payton, on playing hard every single play

"I love football in the rain. That's what it's all about."

—Brian Urlacher, on playing in bad weather

"When I put a good hit on someone, it would excite me for the entire game."

—Mike Singletary, on the thrill of playing aggressive defense

"I got along with Halas just fine. If he'd paid me a little more, I might have even liked him!"

—Doug Atkins, on his owner and coach, who had a reputation for paying low salaries

"If you have the football and eleven guys are after you, if you're smart, you'll run."

—Red Grange, on the "secret" to being a fast runner

"Nobody who ever gave his best regretted it."

—George Halas, on the reward of hard work

"We were convinced that nobody could beat us."

—Jim McMahon, on the Bears during their incredible 1985 season

LEFT: Brian Urlacher doesn't notice the snow as he raises the NFC Championship trophy. **ABOVE**: George Halas goes over a play with assistant coach Clark Shaughnessy.

For the Record

The great Bears teams and players have left their marks on the record books. These are the "best of the best" …

BEARS AWARD WINNERS

WINNER	AWARD	YEAR
Sid Luckman	NFL Player of the Year	1943
Doug Atkins	Pro Bowl Co-MVP	1959
Mike Ditka	NFL Offensive Rookie of the Year*	1961
Ronnie Bull	NFL Offensive Rookie of the Year	1962
George Halas	NFL Coach of the Year	1963
George Halas	NFL Coach of the Year	1965
Gale Sayers	NFL Offensive Rookie of the Year	1965
Gale Sayers	Pro Bowl Co-MVP	1967
Gale Sayers	Pro Bowl Co-MVP	1968
Gale Sayers	Pro Bowl Co-MVP	1970
Wally Chambers	NFL Defensive Rookie of the Year	1973
Walter Payton	NFL Most Valuable Player	1977
Walter Payton	NFL Offensive Player of the Year	1977
Walter Payton	Pro Bowl MVP	1978
Mike Singletary	NFL Defensive Player of the Year	1985
Mike Ditka	NFL Coach of the Year	1985
Richard Dent	Super Bowl XX MVP	1986
Mike Singletary	NFL Defensive Player of the Year	1988
Mark Carrier	NFL Defensive Rookie of the Year	1990
Brian Urlacher	NFL Defensive Rookie of the Year	2000
Dick Jauron	NFL Coach of the Year	2001
Anthony Thomas	NFL Offensive Rookie of the Year	2001
Lovie Smith	NFL Coach of the Year	2005
Brian Urlacher	NFL Defensive Player of the Year	2005

** An award given to the league's best player in his first season.*

Doug Atkins

Walter Payton

BEARS ACHIEVEMENTS

ACHIEVEMENT	YEAR
NFL Champions	1921*
NFL Champions	1932
NFL Western Division Champions	1933
NFL Champions	1933
NFL Western Division Champions	1934
NFL Western Division Champions	1937
NFL Western Division Champions	1940
NFL Champions	1940
NFL Western Division Champions	1941
NFL Champions	1941
NFL Western Division Champions	1942
NFL Western Division Champions	1943
NFL Champions	1943
NFL Western Division Champions	1946
NFL Champions	1946
NFL Western Conference Champions	1956
NFL Western Conference Champions	1963
NFL Champions	1963
NFC Central Champions	1984
NFC Central Champions	1985
NFC Champions	1985
Super Bowl XX Champions	1985**
NFC Central Champions	1987
NFC Central Champions	1988
NFC Central Champions	1990
NFC Central Champions	2001
NFC North Champions	2005
NFC North Champions	2006
NFC Champions	2006

* *Team played as the Chicago Staleys*

** *Super Bowls are played early the following year, but the game is counted as the championship of this season.*

Mark Carrier

Steve McMichael gets a hand from Mike Singletary, the NFL's best defensive player in 1985 and 1988.

Pinpoints

The history of a football team is made up of many smaller stories. These stories take place all over the map—not just in the city a team calls "home." Match the pushpins on these maps to the Team Facts and you will begin to see the story of the Bears unfold!

TEAM FACTS

1 Chicago, Illinois—*The Bears have played here since 1921.*

2 Pittsfield, Massachusetts—*Brian Piccolo was born here.*

3 Connellsville, Pennsylvania—*Johnny Lujack was born here.*

4 Jersey City, New Jersey—*Jim McMahon was born here.*

5 St. Augustine, Florida—*Willie Galimore was born here.*

6 Florence, Alabama—*Harlon Hill was born here.*

7 Columbia, Mississippi—*Walter Payton was born here.*

8 Gladewater, Texas—*Lovie Smith was born here.*

9 Oklahoma City, Oklahoma—*Dan Hampton was born here.*

10 Wichita, Kansas—*Gale Sayers was born here.*

11 Pasco, Washington—*Brian Urlacher was born here.*

12 Rainy River, Ontario, Canada—*Bronko Nagurski was born here.*

Harlon Hill

Play Ball

Football is a sport played by two teams on a field that is 100 yards long. The game is divided into four 15-minute quarters. Each team must have 11 players on the field at all times. The group that has the ball is called the offense. The group trying to keep the offense from moving the ball forward is called the defense.

A football game is made up of a series of "plays." Each play starts and ends with a referee's signal. A play begins when the center snaps the ball between his legs to the quarterback. The quarterback then gives the ball to a teammate, throws (or "passes") the ball to a teammate, or runs with the ball himself. The job of the defense is to tackle the player with the ball or stop the quarterback's pass. A play ends when the ball (or player holding the ball) is "down." The offense must move the ball forward at least 10 yards every four downs. If it fails to do so, the other team is given the ball. If the offense has not made 10 yards after three downs—and does not want to risk losing the ball—it can kick (or "punt") the ball to make the other team start from its own end of the field.

At each end of a football field is a goal line, which divides the field from the end zone. A team must run or pass the ball over the goal line to score a touchdown, which counts for six points. After scoring a touchdown, a team can try a short kick for one "extra point," or try again to run or pass across the goal line for two points. Teams can score three points from anywhere on the field by kicking the ball between the goalposts. This is called a field goal.

The defense can score two points if it tackles a player while he is in his own end zone. This is called a safety. The defense can also score points by taking the ball away from the offense and crossing the opposite goal line for a touchdown. The team with the most points after 60 minutes is the winner.

Football may seem like a very hard game to understand, but the more you play and watch football, the more "little things" you are likely to notice. The next time you are at a game, look for these plays:

PLAY LIST

BLITZ—A play where the defense sends extra tacklers after the quarterback. If the quarterback sees a blitz coming, he passes the ball quickly. If he does not, he can end up at the bottom of a very big pile!

DRAW—A play where the offense pretends it will pass the ball, and then gives it to a running back. If the offense can "draw" the defense to the quarterback and his receivers, the running back should have lots of room to run.

FLY PATTERN—A play where a team's fastest receiver is told to "fly" past the defensive backs for a long pass. Many long touchdowns are scored on this play.

SQUIB KICK—A play where the ball is kicked a short distance on purpose. A squib kick is used when the team kicking off does not want the other team's fastest player to catch the ball and run with it.

SWEEP—A play where the ball carrier follows a group of teammates moving sideways to "sweep" the defense out of the way. A good sweep gives the runner a chance to gain a lot of yards before he is tackled or forced out of bounds.

Glossary

FOOTBALL WORDS TO KNOW

AMERICAN PROFESSIONAL FOOTBALL ASSOCIATION (APFA)—The league that began in 1920 and became the National Football League in 1922.

BLOCKING—Protection of the ball carrier by his teammates.

DIVISION—A group of teams (within a league) that all play in the same part of the country.

DRAFTED—Chosen from a group of the best college players. The NFL draft is held each spring.

DRIVE—A series of plays by the offense that "drives" the defense back toward its own goal line.

EXHIBITION TOUR—A series of games played for the entertainment of fans in different cities. The games do not count on a team's official record.

FUMBLING—Dropping the ball as it is being carried.

HALL OF FAME—The museum in Canton, Ohio, where football's greatest players are honored. A player voted into the Hall of Fame is sometimes called a "Hall of Famer."

INCOMPLETE PASS—A pass that hits the ground before it is caught.

INTERCEPTION—A pass that is caught by the defensive team.

INTERFERED—Illegally prevented a receiver from catching a pass.

LINEMEN—Players who begin each down crouched at the line of scrimmage.

NATIONAL CHAMPIONSHIP—The honor given to college football's top-ranked team.

NATIONAL FOOTBALL CONFERENCE (NFC)—One of two groups of teams that make up the National Football League. The winner of the NFC plays the winner of the American Football Conference (AFC) in the Super Bowl.

NATIONAL FOOTBALL LEAGUE (NFL)—The league that started in 1920 and is still operating today.

NFL CHAMPIONSHIP—The game played to decide the winner of the league each year from 1933 to 1969.

NORTH DIVISION—A division for teams that play in the northern part of the country. The Bears play in the NFC North.

PLAYER-COACH—A player who also coaches the team.

PLAYOFFS—The games played after the season to determine which teams play in the Super Bowl.

PRO BOWL—The NFL's all-star game, played after the Super Bowl.

PROFESSIONAL—A player or team that plays a sport for money. College players are not paid, so they are considered "amateurs."

ROOKIE—A player in his first season.

SUPER BOWL—The championship of football, played between the winners of the NFC and AFC.

OTHER WORDS TO KNOW

ASSEMBLED—Put together.

CANVAS—A heavy, strong cloth.

DECADE—A period of 10 years; also a specific period, such as the 1950s.

GRAMMY AWARD—An honor given to people in the music industry.

HUNCH—A feeling that something is going to happen.

INTENSE—Very strong or very deep.

LIGAMENTS—Bands of tissue that connect bones.

OLYMPICS—An international sports competition held every four years.

PERSISTENT—Refusing to give up.

SEARING—Hot enough to burn the skin.

SENSATION—The cause of excitement.

SPLICED—Added to film or tape.

TAILBONE—The bone that protects the base of the spine.

TRADITION—A belief or custom that is handed down from generation to generation.

Places to Go

ON THE ROAD

CHICAGO BEARS
1410 South Museum Campus Drive
Chicago, Illinois 60605
(847) 295-6600

THE PRO FOOTBALL HALL OF FAME
2121 George Halas Drive NW
Canton, Ohio 44708
(330) 456-8207

ON THE WEB

THE NATIONAL FOOTBALL LEAGUE — www.nfl.com
- *Learn more about the National Football League*

THE CHICAGO BEARS — www.chicagobears.com
- *Learn more about the Chicago Bears*

THE PRO FOOTBALL HALL OF FAME — www.profootballhof.com
- *Learn more about football's greatest players*

ON THE BOOKSHELF

To learn more about the sport of football, look for these books at your library or bookstore:

- Fleder, Rob–Editor. *The Football Book.* New York, NY: Sports Illustrated Books, 2005.
- Kennedy, Mike. *Football.* Danbury, CT: Franklin Watts, 2003.
- Savage, Jeff. *Play by Play Football.* Minneapolis, MN: Lerner Sports, 2004.

Index

PAGE NUMBERS IN **BOLD** REFER TO ILLUSTRATIONS.

The Team

MARK STEWART has written more than 20 books on football, and over 100 sports books for kids. He grew up in New York City during the 1960s rooting for the Giants and Jets, and now takes his two daughters, Mariah and Rachel, to watch them play in their home state of New Jersey. Mark comes from a family of writers. His grandfather was Sunday Editor of *The New York Times* and his mother was Articles Editor of *The Ladies' Home Journal* and *McCall's*. Mark has profiled hundreds of athletes over the last 20 years. He has also written several books about New York and New Jersey. Mark is a graduate of Duke University, with a degree in History. He lives with his daughters and wife Sarah overlooking Sandy Hook, New Jersey.

JASON AIKENS is the Collections Curator at the Pro Football Hall of Fame. He is responsible for the preservation of the Pro Football Hall of Fame's collection of artifacts and memorabilia and obtaining new donations of memorabilia from current players and NFL teams. Jason has a Bachelor of Arts in History from Michigan State University and a Master's in History from Western Michigan University where he concentrated on sports history. Jason has been working for the Pro Football Hall of Fame since 1997; before that he was an intern at the College Football Hall of Fame. Jason's family has roots in California and has been following the St. Louis Rams since their days in Los Angeles, California. He lives with his wife Cynthia and recent addition to the team Angelina in Canton, Ohio.